PIE-BITER

by

Ruthanne Lum McCunn

Illustrated by You-shan Tang

For
Arthurita Drysdale
Robin Grossman
and
Chu Moon Ho

Pie-Biter
by Ruthanne Lum McCunn
Illustrated by You-shan Tang

Chinese language edition translated by
Ellen Lai-shan Yeung

Library of Congress Catalog Card Number: 83-70042

ENGLISH LANGUAGE EDITION   ISBN 0-932538-09-6
CHINESE LANGUAGE EDITION   ISBN 0-932538-10-X
> $11.95

Design Enterprises of San Francisco
P.O. Box 14695
San Francisco, CA 94114

Printed in Japan

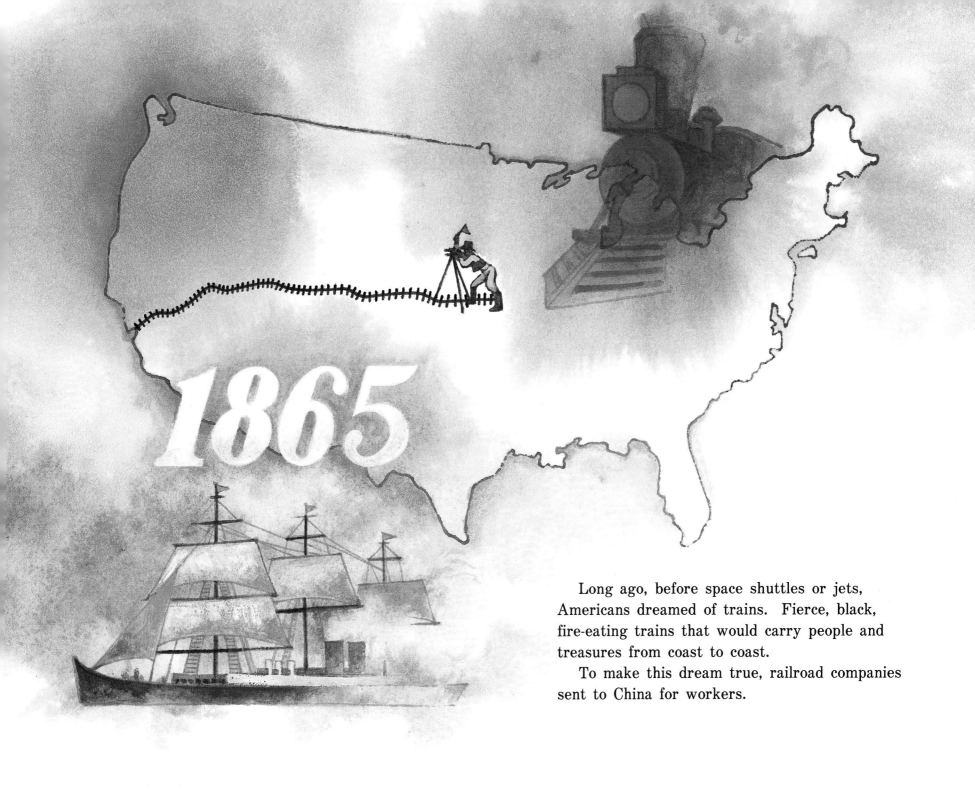

Long ago, before space shuttles or jets, Americans dreamed of trains. Fierce, black, fire-eating trains that would carry people and treasures from coast to coast.

To make this dream true, railroad companies sent to China for workers.

Hundreds, thousands of men crossed the Ocean of Peace to build the iron road America needed. Among them was Hoi, a boy with smiling face atop a body thin as a bamboo pole.

Work on the iron road was hard and dangerous. The hours between morning and evening rice stretched long and hungry.

Hoi's smile disappeared, and he became too weak to work.

"My stomach is shouting for food," he complained.

"A cup of tea will quiet its growling," the tea carrier said.

But the cup of steaming hot tea could not satisfy Hoi.
"I need rice."
"You cannot hold a bowl, chopsticks, and pick axe too," the gang boss scolded.

Hoi thought a moment. "No, but I can hold a
pie in my left hand and swing the axe with my
right."

"Pie?"

Hoi smiled. "American pie."

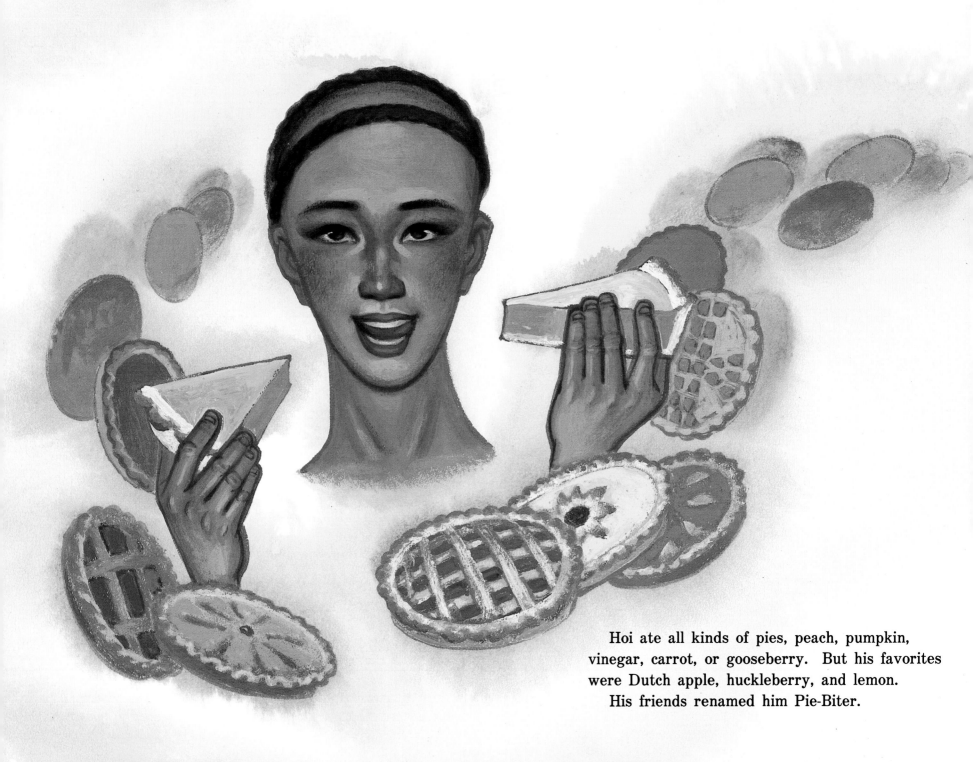

Hoi ate all kinds of pies, peach, pumpkin, vinegar, carrot, or gooseberry. But his favorites were Dutch apple, huckleberry, and lemon. His friends renamed him Pie-Biter.

Pie-Biter's body thickened, becoming as hard as the rails he laid. And when a job needed extra strength, the men called for him.

"Pie-Biter, lower me over the cliff so I can drill a hole for explosives," the dynamiter said.

"Pie-Biter, dig us out," the men buried in the avalanche cried.

"Pie-Biter, lift that fallen pine," the gang boss ordered.

Then, after three years of labor, the rails from West and East met.

"The iron road is finished," the gang boss said. "There's no more work for us here."

While the company bosses celebrated, the men made plans.

"My parents are old," the tea carrier said. "I will take my savings and sail for home."

"I will follow new gold strikes
north," the dynamiter said.

"I will start a boarding house, then
send for my wife and children," the
cook decided.

"And you, Pie-Biter, what will you do?" the gang boss asked.

"I will buy a train."

He laughed at the men's astonished faces. "A train of horses that can pack supplies into camps far from the iron road."

"But you know nothing of horses," the dynamiter said.

"I will learn."

Pie-Biter asked for a job with Spanish Louie's pack train.

"I will cook in exchange for lessons about horses," he said.

Spanish Louie shook Pie-Biter's hand. "Agreed."

At first, Pie-Biter found himself tangled in
harness, halters, and pack ropes.

The horses fooled him by puffing up their
bellies when he tried to tighten their cinches.
Then their packs slipped,
sometimes tumbling into deep canyons.

Finally, after many months, Spanish Louie spoke the words Pie-Biter had been working and waiting for. "There's nothing more I can teach you. You're ready to run your own pack train."

Pie-Biter bought ten short-backed horses with thick bodies and strong, sturdy legs. He ordered two boxes specially made, one for either side of his saddle. Then, into each box, he stacked eight pies.

He was ready to go.

Except for one thing.

He had no freight.

"No one trusts a greenhorn," Spanish Louie explained.

"But I am a good packer. You said so yourself."

Spanish Louie pointed to the merchants. "You must make them believe."

Pie-Biter took out a pie and munched it thoughtfully. How could he prove he was a good packer if the merchants didn't give him a chance?

He finished the pie and reached for another.

Then another.

And another.

When he had eaten all sixteen pies, Pie-Biter said to Spanish Louie. "The three biggest pack trains in this town are yours, Ah Choy's and Sleepy Kan's. If all of you go on holiday at the same time, the merchants will have to use me to carry their freight."

Spanish Louie chuckled. "I will be happy to take two week's rest, but how will you persuade Ah Choy and Sleepy Kan to stop packing too?"

"I have a plan."

Dressed in his best, Pie-Biter called on Ah Choy.

"Good news," Pie-Biter said. "China's armies have won many battles against the barbarians."

"What has that to do with me?" Ah Choy said impatiently.

Pie-Biter unrolled a long paper heavy with seals of office. "The Emperor instructs us to celebrate the victories with two weeks of rest."

"But I have hundreds of pounds of rice and flour and sugar that I have promised to deliver."

Pie-Biter shook the paper. "You dare disobey an order from the Son of Heaven?"

"No, of course not," Ah Choy stammered. "The merchants can wait."

Next, Pie-Biter called on Sleepy Kan.
"I willingly obey the Emperor," he yawned.

Without Spanish Louie, Ah Choy, or Sleepy Kan, the merchants had to hire Pie-Biter. And for the next two weeks, his horses forded streams and scrambled over boulders while Pie-Biter munched his favorite pies and the canyons echoed with his songs. He did not lose so much as one egg.

When Ah Choy discovered he had been tricked, he was furious.

But Sleepy Kan laughed. "There's plenty of work for us all."

Over the next fifteen years, Pie-Biter's string of horses doubled, then trebled. He became a rich man with many hired helpers.

But he nibbled at pies without enjoyment. He did not sing.

"What is wrong?" Spanish Louie asked his friend.

"I am lonely for my father and mother and brothers," Pie-Biter said. "I want a wife and a son of my own."

The next day, Pie-Biter led his pack train to Spanish Louie's. "My horses have served me well. Now they will serve you. I am going home."

Then he bought a one-way ticket on a steamship bound for China. He ordered fifty pies to be delivered on board.

No one in America saw or heard from Pie-Biter again. But for many years, travellers from China spoke of pie shops in villages and market towns. And the flavors they served were Pie-Biter's favorites.

Pie-Biter lived and worked in the Pacific Northwest for twenty years. Pioneers preserved his story orally, and Fern Cable Trull recorded it in her unpublished masters thesis, "The History of the Chinese in Idaho from 1864-1910" (University of Oregon, 1946).

About the Author:

Ruthanne Lum McCunn is an Amerasian born in San Francisco's Chinatown. When she was one year old, her family returned to Hong Kong where she attended both Chinese and English schools. At the age of sixteen, she returned to America to begin her college education.

Since graduation, Ms. McCunn has worked as a children's librarian, elementary school teacher, bilingual/bicultural junior and senior high school teacher.

She is the author of "An Illustrated History of the Chinese in America," and "Thousand Pieces of Gold," the first biographical novel of a Chinese-American pioneer woman.

About the Illustrator:

You-shan Tang is a graduate of Central Art Academy and Peking University, trained in literature as well as art. A firm believer that an alliance between western and Chinese art will lead to new artistic dimensions, he blends Asian and occidental techniques into a harmonious fusion. Though this book is predominantly western in tone, traditional Chinese techniques can be seen in the bold expressive strokes, fine line drawings, and decorative motifs.